Erotica Short Stories with Explicit Sex to Read in Bed

Cheeky Girls…

My Lip-biting Short Stories Series
- Book One -

Alex Frack

ACKNOWLEDGMENTS

'My Lip-Biting Short Stories' is a tested series of book for women, men and couples looking for classic easy-to-read erotica and sex stories for women with very explicit sex scenes.

Think about it. Don't we all need nice, steamy and sexy short stories that can be read in bed, right before sleeping to finish our day with a little bit of privacy and fun? Or even first thing in the morning to spice up your day, not to mention those long and boring commuting journeys where a little bit of sexy can... Well, you know.

Cheeky Girls...' is the first volume in the series and proposes four short sex & erotica stories that will make you bite your lips. Perhaps even more...

The first story - Cheeky Melina - will get you into the universe of two girlfriends who, more than sharing a flat, happen to share a lip-biting dose of friendship, complicity and cheekiness when a boyfriend passes by.

The second story - Today was a bad day - will

rather get you into the life of an anonymous girl who, one night, decides to let go and allows her lover to take control.

The third story - Girls Night In - will get you into one of those girls' evenings where gossips and no taboo speaking can lead to surprising development. The only boy there might remember that evening for a long while...

As per the other book in this series, this short stories book is not about romance. The short stories build on love and cheeky needs but go straight to the point and contain very explicit sex scenes. They are written to be read easily and rapidly, in five to ten minutes, again and again.

If you are looking for a little bit of selfish sexy fun every once in a while, my book was made for you!

Oh, but of course reading them out-loud is also an option if you are not alone ... Your choice!

Last but not least, don't forget to join my mailing list! I will use it to let you know about my future book releases (and subscribers get one of my unpublished sexy stories for free…). Here is the link:

http://eepurl.com/cQtD_1

Cheekily yours...

Alex.

1 CHEEKY MELINA …

Two o'clock in the morning, the entrance door slams. My roommate Melina returns home with her lover, without taking too many precautions.

For her defense, I told her that I would be away from home this weekend to visit my family in the countryside. But then, a strike later, my plans have been canceled and I find myself at home, alone with my university work and my revisions.

Anyway, Melina and Jonathan seem to make themselves at home. Melina laughs and, given the way she expresses herself, I reach the conclusion that these two will not let me go to sleep again.

I get up and put on a tee-shirt before opening my door quietly. Melina and Jonathan are in the corridor, glued to each other. He wears some classy shirt and beige trousers but turns his back to me. She wears a pretty black dress that shows-off her delicate shapes and enhances her waist. And she clearly notices me.

Her hands gently slide in Jonathan's neck to make him look away from me, her tongue even slides into his mouth as she playfully winks at me. Slowly but surely, his hands fall down her waist, grab her butt. She laughs, calls him a cheeky boy and drags him towards her room, winking at me.

Minutes pass, Melina and Jonathan are still in the corridor. He caresses her, she moans softly, laughs and seems to enjoy her lover's attention. But Jonathan, who knows the apartment, decides to play it safe. He turns his head towards my door, considers the dark.

"Honey, where is Karine?"

Melina gets her hands in his neck again, starts to kiss him deeply to get his attention back.

"Shhh, forget about her ..."

"But you'll wake her up if you keep laughing and moaning like that ..."

Melina opens her eyes wide and looks shocked.

"What? I don't... moan!"

I smile, finding this young man very considerate towards me and this girl definitely cheeky. She slaps his arm with a smile.

"Forget about her, Karine has gone on a family weekend, we won't be waking her ..."

Melina' answer makes me smile. She and I have been roommates for a few years now and, before that, we were friends in high school. We talk about everything, without complex. On occasion, I must confess that we happened to share our bed, even a handsome young man. Hmmm, thinking about it ... Ouch, my lip!

Anyway, Melina is a sassy girl who lets me know, very innocently, that I am authorized to enjoy the show. So, when the two lovers finally enter her room, I quietly get out of mine and approach in silence.

Melina, as I expected, has left her door slightly open. In the dark, I lean against the doorframe. Melina is undressing, about a meter away from Jonathan who happens to be sitting on the bed. She stays in front of him, lets her little dress fall down her arms and down her legs, revealing a set of slightly transparent black lingerie as well as black stockings. Melina then removes her bra and gently throws it to her man's face before hiding her small chest with her forearm.

Captivated, I am still leaning against the doorframe, watching in silence and biting my lips. I am taking root.

Jonathan grabs his girl's hips and draws her to him. He now seems to be playing with her breasts, his hands holding her very cute and firm butt before slowly pulling her panties down. When these reach the floor, she simply moves one step towards him, in silence.

With a gentle gesture, he kisses her tummy and makes her turn around until she faces the door. And me. He bends slightly to cover the pretty brunette's back with kisses while letting his hands run on her adorable breasts. She, of course, faces me with a smirk and hides her bikini line with a hand and an innocent look on her face.

Jonathan gets up, slips his left hand between her sexy legs while the other covers her chest. His fingers gently slide inside Melina, who now closes her eyes and moans, still facing me, while his right hand gently caresses her brown nipples. Then Jonathan makes her turn and sit on the bed. He undresses without taking his eyes off her. She crosses her legs and looks at him. A furtive glance towards the door, she knows that I am not losing a beat of this.

Jonathan kneels, kisses Melina and begins to nibble on her chest. I imagine his teeth closing on the girl's perfect breasts, his tongue gently circling her tits to make her react. *Hmmm, why am I not getting any of that! It's so unfair!*

Melina's hands gently get into his hair, then guide his head, down. Jonathan obeys without saying a word, and a few moments later finds himself nibbling on Melina's wide open inner tights.

Jonathan's head hides the pretty brunette but I have no doubt about what he does. Melina looks at me, moaning and biting her lower lip as Jonathan's mouth runs inside her legs. She smiles, seems delighted. She watches her lover eat her with envy and passion while caressing his hair and guiding him deeper. I imagine his tongue opening her, and bite my lips as she finally collapses on her bed, wide open, her feet on Jonathan's shoulders, at the mercy of his never-ending licks and bites.

Leaning against the frame of the door, I take advantage of the spectacle. My fingers run down my stomach, I play a little bit with my tits too. *Hmmm ... I'm never going to resist this…*

Then a scream. The beautiful brunette's body

arches. Melina turns around on the bed. On her four, she presents her hips to him who, imperturbable, grabs her butt to immobilize her and continues to eat her, from behind. Melina tries to stop Jonathan, her right hand looks for him, passes through his hair, tries to take position between his tongue and her burning pussy, visibly unable to resist the intensity of the caress anymore.

"Honey, wait ..."

"What?"

"Take your time..."

"You don't like it?"

"I love it! Just ..."

Jonathan ignores her, goes on, tastes her, eats her. Melina moans, turns again and lays down on her back, pressing Jonathan's face between her thighs, her body arching. Jonathan looks up, smiles at her with complicity.

In the corridor, the heat rises. My left hand just plunged into my panties, I feel wet, ready to play.

"What's the problem then?"

Melina, her legs wide open in front of me, passes her hands through Jonathan's hair and gets up. She whispers a "sit down" and goes to the door to grab a hair clip on the chest of drawers. Naked, facing me, dressed in her simple black stockings with her small breasts visibly excited, Melina looks at me in silence, catches her breath. I wink at her to show her that I did not lose a second of this infernal show, she responds with a smile and then ties her hair, proudly showing her chest and her naked body, before turning again to Jonathan.

A few seconds later, the roles are reversed. Jonathan sits, Melina kneels between his legs so as not to block my sight. She passes her hand on her man's boxers, then takes them down. Her hands take possession of Jonathan's manhood, which now stretches energetically.

Clean-shaven, his cock is hard, proud. But

Jonathan is totally absorbed and of course does not notice the roommate who discreetly observes him by the opening of the door, in the dark. I do not lose a beat of this spectacle, even bite my lip thinking about the fun I could have if I was her, feeling him inside my mouth. My fingers are agitated; I do not already stand in place. *Hmmmm, why am I not having this man?!*

Melina sticks to Jonathan, speaks softly has she holds his hard cock between her small breasts. Their faces brush against each other, Melina crosses her feet underneath her, laughing and squirming between his legs, and occasionally making him moan with a treat.

Melina's head then began to come and go on Jonathan's hard cock. My hand continued to slide on my breasts, then on my stomach and again between my thighs.

Melina bent her head to the side, kissing her lover's stomach while holding him firmly in one of her hands. Then, always aside, Melina took Jonathan in her mouth again, making

21

sure that I could enjoy the show. Gently, but languorously and deeper, Melina's mouth and tongue took possession of Jonathan as her hands came and went on him. Jonathan seemed to discover the oral talents of his girl and quickly appeared to have more and more difficulty resisting her. But Melina seemed to appreciate the exercise and, imperturbable, kept playing with that gorgeous stick I was now jealous of ... *Please let me come and play too, I'll be a very good girl, I promise…*

My panties then became soaked and burning, making my discreet presence more and more complicated. When Melina decided to climb on her man and impaled on his generously stretched cock, I decided to slip away, not without watching a few seconds the deep and wet come and go movement that made Melina moan.

When I got to my room, I closed my door in silence and pulled out my tee-shirt and panties. Finally naked, I slipped under my cover while listening to the cheeky Melina who was now starting to moan loudly. Her hands rested on the wall separating our rooms, and I could hear and feel their moves on it. It felt like I was actually in the room with them. Gently opening my thighs, I started indulging myself with silent, intimate, deep and wet caresses. First, spread the lips, caress this swollen button, imagine Melina impaled on this cock. Then imagine that my pussy too is filled with a deliciously tense member. *Hmmm, biiigg….* Caress those delicate lips and then gently push my fingers deep inside me, listening to them as they make love.

Then Jonathan also began to moan. Melina's hands moved onto the wall, the bed squeaked. Melina hit her bedhead as I imagined Jonathan standing behind her. His cock now had to be nested deep inside her. Melina no longer held back her moans. The creaking of the bed accelerated, Jonathan's thrusts as well.

Then Melina received a frank slap on the butt, sonorous and suggestive, and began to truly give voice, hiding my own moans.

The idea of Jonathan behind her, pounding

her, made me crazy. I imagined myself, grabbed and fucked brutally. Then Melina screamed, her hands clenched on the wall. At the same time, Jonathan also groaned and I felt jealous as I thought about her body being flooded with his pleasure. My fingers inside me did the rest.

After these three simultaneous orgasms, calm returned, and the whispers of the two lovers quickly gave way to the silence of the night, which for me was sweet and beautiful. The next morning, at about ten o'clock, my phone vibrated. A message from Melina, who most naturally wished me a pleasant Sunday, hoping that my night had been as pleasant as hers. Cheeky Melina…

2 | TODAY WAS A BAD DAY

Today was a bad day, the kind of day that starts with an argument and ends with bad moods. Jeff and I have been together for six months now, and today was our first fight. A sex fight!

See, I'm a pretty tough girl. I know, I can be difficult for people to manage but I have my moods. And in the bedroom, I like to be on top. I like to give the rhythm, I like being in control, I don't like letting guys decide. I never let the guys decide. I never did.

Anyway, this morning, Jeff woke me up with cuddles. Hmm, he was so sweet... his hands... got me upside down in no time, and

I got on top of him. Except he took it wrong this time. He got upset, told me I had to let him handle things sometimes. That pretty much turned us off and we went into a fight.

I spent my day thinking about it, wondered why I do keep coming on top of men. Not that I've had so much of them but, truly enough, I'm not sure I ever let go with a man... *Damn...*

Anyway, when I came back home tonight, Jeff was grumpy, barely gave me a kiss on the cheek. And now he is watching TV, slouched on the couch like I'm not even here... and I'm thinking that after all, he's probably right. I need to let go...

I chew my lips, I'm not sure why, but I'm stressed. *Go on girl! Move! Let the man do, don't be stupid!*

I stand, probably a bit abruptly because Jeff jumps.

"where are you going?"

I'm not answering, just looking at him over my shoulder and moving to our bedroom. *I need something better than those jeans and jumper.*

How about… hmm, black tights? Black thong…
Bra? No bra…

"Jeff? Can you come over for a minute please?"

"I'm kinda busy right now…"

"Please!"

Jeff moves, comes along. I'm in the middle of the door, my right hand holding my breasts. He fixes me, looks at my chest, at my thong, then he looks for my eyes, expecting something.

"How about…" I'm shivering. "How about… we start over but this time… you have me the way you like?"

Jeff looks into my eyes.

"My way?"

"Yes…"

"No interference?"

I nod.

"Your way, no interference."

He smiles, seems interested. Then he tells me to turn around with a hand movement, no speaking. I obey and turn around. His hands touch my back, up my spine. I shiver again. He comes closer, whispers in my ear...

"Hands down..."

I obey, get my hands down, release my breasts. He opens a drawer, gets my favorite blue hair ribbons, tickles my shoulders with it, lets it run down my arms... he then crosses my wrists, ties them together with it. *I get the message, you're in charge now...*

His hands get on me, he is behind me, holds me. My back, my sides, my... *hmm*... my boobs. He seems to be decided to play it a little rough, grabs my breasts fully in his hands.

"Hey, slow..."

"Shh, we said my way, right?"

"I... ok."

His foot gets between my feet, he makes me

open my legs. I shiver, trying to get used to being a good girl. He grabs my neck, gently but firmly, and pushes me to the bed.

"So, who's in control?"

"... Jeff"

"Say again?"

"... Jeff... is in control"

"Good girl..."

He gets me on the bed, on my four, slaps my butt.

"Ouch!"... *hmmm, ok...*

He slaps my butt again. *Hmmm.*

"A problem perhaps?"

"I... no."

I feel his eyes on me, on my butt, on my thong. His hands take possession of me. His fingers run down my leg, then between my legs, he makes me moan, I bite my lips. His fingers run on the silk of my thong. *Oh my, he is driving me crazy!*

He spanks me again. I moan, then blush. Can't control it… He pulls my hair gently, makes a ponytail, holds it firmly. *That's a first…* His other hand then moves on my back, on my sides. He grabs my boobs roughly; I bite my lips to stop a moan. His fingers play with my tits, they make small circles, they make me feel tense, excited, as my tits harden.

I moan, he stops. *No, please don't stop!*

"Jeff…" *Please continue…*

My butt gets spanked once more. I get the message.

He moves back, starts to kiss my back, down my spine, his hands grab my waist, then my butt, he pulls my thong on the side, then half-way down my tights. I can feel his eyes on my pussy, I move a little bit, uncomfortable with the situation. But he keeps me there. I can feel his breath on my skin, he's so close… *Give it a kiss, come on baby, kiss it…*

No kiss, but a finger slides inside me. I moan, move my leg. He keeps me there tight, his finger taking possession of me… in, out. *God, why did I wait so long to let a man do this to me? What's wrong with me?*

Two fingers in, my legs feel electric, I can't resist, moan a little louder. But he stops, suddenly, and bites my butt.

"Ouch!"

"Shhhh."

He turns around the bed, comes in front of me, looks at me as I'm still on my four, my thong still halfway down my tights. He opens his jeans, lets them fall on the floor and looks at me.

"Remind me, honey, how are we doing this?"

I look into his eyes, tied, his girl.

"Your way…"

"Hmm, good girl, come here."

I move closer, slowly, with my hands still tied up, and watch him pull his boxers down. His cock pops, not hard but close to it. He brings the head of his cock to my lips.

"Give it a kiss honey."

I obey, kiss the tip of his cock.

"Go on, I want to feel your mouth all over me."

I look up, his hand gets into my hair to guide me. I open my mouth, lets him bring the head of his cock on my tongue. I close my eyes. *God, he is… hmm.*

His hand makes another ponytail with my hair, he pushes his cock inside my mouth as my lips close on him. His hands move on me, he grabs my tits again, pulls them, teases them before making me sit on the edge of the bed. Then he takes my mouth again, makes me play. My tongue dances on his shaft, twirls around his head. I feel him, his hardness, his reactions. *Oh my, I love it…* My left-hand cups his balls softly, my fingers play with them, my tongue moves down his shaft as he guides me to his balls.

"Go on baby, don't stop…"

I take his cock in my right hand, as much as I can since the ribbon is still restricting my moves. I stroke it gently as I take his balls in my mouth, one after the other. I moan, look up at him with a smile. He grabs his shaft, guides it into my mouth again, pushes it all the way down. I gag… *Ouch!* In again, deeper in my mouth, down my throat, until my lips reach his base. He holds me, releases me. *My god, that was another first…* He starts over, moves in, moves out… fucks my mouth, his way…

A drop appears from the tip of his cock as I catch my breath, he looks at me. I let my tongue run, make the drop disappear. I stare at him, silent. *Are you happy now?*

"Hmmm, what a good girl…'

He pushes me on the bed, takes my thong down my legs, opens me up widely. I blush, not really into letting guys eat me out but… *Hmmm, that mouth on me, my god. Ok!, come on!*

Do it!

His hands keep me wide open, he explores my pussy, spreads my lips, suckles on my clit. My fingers get into his hair.

"Let me handle that hun, relax, ok?"

He knows I'm not comfortable but keeps playing, bites me gently, eats me up. I moan. His fingers get inside me, my head flips back, my back arches. His hands brushing against my inner tights make me moan louder, then he grabs my boobs again as his tongue runs inside my pussy.

"God! Jeff!!"

"How's my way hun?"

His tongue slides inside me with his finger, I scream.

"Jeff, please, I'm getting crazy, I…"

"Shhh, my girl, my way…"

My tied hands caress my breasts, he pushes them away.

"Hands above your head"

I obey, get my hands on top of my head. *He's going to kill me!!* He moves on me, makes sure the ribbon keeps me tied up. His hard cock touches my face, he grabs the back of my neck, slides his shaft inside my mouth again. *Fuck, I didn't know he loved my mouth that much...* Deep, again, then merely offers me his head to play with.

Our eyes meet, his hand runs down on my tummy. His fingers get inside my legs, he makes me open up again and invades my pussy like never. *Oh, my, god.*

"Now baby, I'm going to fuck that pussy, as much as I want, my way, my pace..."

I moan, gently letting my teeth meet his cock, fighting for that little bit of control I have left. He slaps my butt, forces his cock down my mouth again, till my lips reach his base. I moan, nod, give up so he releases me, pushes me back, stands in front of me and puts his hard cock on my landing strip. I bite my bottom lip, he's maintaining his control on me...

But then he flips me around, grabs my hips, gets me on my four again. *No, not doggy style, he knows I...*

"Jeff! No! You know I'm not..."

"My girl, my way..."

I grab the pillows. *I've never been into doggy sex, he knows it!* His cock pushes, gets inside my pussy lips. He moans loudly, I scream. *He's so deep!!!* My toes curl up, my legs get electric. I can feel his cock big and hard in my tiny me. *He...'s about to ... make me cum! Ok I love it! Fuck me baby!!!*

But he slows down, right when I was getting there! He moves in and out gently.

"Jeff... no..."

"What?"

"I was..."

"What? Say it!"

"Jeff..."

"Say it!!" He slaps my butt again, moves even more slowly inside me. He wants me to give him full control. *You wish! I won't say it.*

He caresses my back gently. My skin is electric, I'm getting totally crazy.

"Don't torture me!"

"What?" *Right, let's do this.*

I look over my shoulder, look at him, straight in the eyes.

"Make me cum, please…"

"Didn't hear you". *He's playing me! Bitch!*

"Jeff!!! Fuck the hell out of me!!!"

He starts to move again inside me. But not hard enough. He's not done playing.

"Someone's learning how to give up control, aren't you?"

I grab my pillow and scream into it. *Fuck my damn pussy!!!*

"Jeeeeeff!"

He spanks me. *Hmmm. Again.*

"More!!"

He spanks me again, twice! My body is screaming. *I am about to have an orgasm.*

"Jeff, I… beg you…"

He moves a little faster, gets harder inside me.

"What darling?"

I look up over my shoulder, stick my eyes into his.

"Will you please fuck me?" *I can't believe I said it. Damn, it feels good.*

He grabs my hips. Digs his cock deep inside me. I pull my pillow, dig my face into it, screaming. He pounds me, his balls hit me.

I am about to yell. Jeff takes my shoulders firmly and gives the last thrust. My body explodes, my brain blasts. I give up, let a yell escape. My body collapses on the bed, Jeff moans, cums inside me, holding me very tight as he fills me with loads of him. I move slightly, try to get him into my arms, but he kisses my shoulder instead and escapes with a wink, letting me naked, my hands tied, out of breath, my tights covered with him. His girl, his way. *Hmmm, today was really a bad day…*

3 | GIRLS NIGHT IN

Tonight is girls night. A good bottle of red wine on the table (a French Saint-Estèphe which turns to exceed our humble expectations), some nice food on the table and a little bit of music in the back to relax after a long day of group shopping.

Mary, the blonde of the group, wears a stunning blue dress bought during the afternoon after many hesitations, along with a swimsuit and a rather sexy underwear set. Cath is the pretty red-haired girl who, despite being very shy, looks like an irresistible fatal woman. And I, Berenice, am the brunette of the band. The girls say I'm pretty and feminine, but the reality is that I have been single for little while now single.

As the evening unfolds and the Saint-Estèphe bottle of wine empties, hearts open and tongues loosen. We talk a lot, gossip even more, laugh and tease each other. A great girls' night in!

Mary, with her rather frank and direct nature, whines about her bitchy beautiful classmate and complains that her last lover did not stay in her bed long enough. These two used to take a malicious pleasure to wake their neighbors regularly, especially me. *Well, their separation is definitely not a loss.*

Cath brags about her red hair and ends up telling us how much her man loves spending time playing with her landing strip which, by the way, is impeccable at all time. You never know, if he feels like getting under her skirts…

Me, well. Nothing much to brag about. Guys have not been looking at anything down there and, in fact, my bikini line looks pretty much like a jungle at the moment.

Later in the evening arrives Lucas, my roommate and best friend, who also turns out to be the only authorized guy in the group.

Inevitably, the evening takes a new turn. Amused by the frankness of our discussions, he joins the game and accepts to tell us about his life. No girlfriend around, no particular one night stand to mention. *No bragging? Come on, cute as he is I don't buy that...* He however agreed with Cath's opinion on the importance of controlled hair growth, and in no time a discussion begins between him and the shy red-head.

"How do you deal with the balls by the way?"

Lucas laughs, Mary rolls her eyes and joins the discussion without giving Lucas a chance to answer.

"Are you going to ask Lucas to show his balls while we're at it?!"

"Oh, come on Mary, I'm the shy one here, don't be prudish ..."

Lucas goes on, laughing, and points his finger at Cath very seriously.

"You know what? I'll show you everything if you show me your fabulous red landing strip!"

Mary rolls her eyes again and looks at Cath.

"You've drunk too much guys..."

Silence. Then Mary continues with a provocative smile.

"Ok, Cath, let's see. If I suck Lucas, would you have some fun watching? Listen to yourselves guys! Don't be ridiculous, come on..."

Silence. Then Cath and Lucas burst-out laughing, jumping-up and shouting.

"Deal!!"

They look at Mary with a clapping high-five, then slowly start to unbutton their shirts and pants. Lucas unzip his jeans, Cath offers a beautiful view on her bra while Mary incredulously shakes her head from left to right with a desperate sigh.

A couple of minutes later, three pairs of eyes focus on Cath, who has visibly lost all shyness and proudly shows off her red landing strip. Impeccably trimmed, indeed. All eyes then turn to Lucas, how is now blushing. Mary now seems very interested in the game, Cath seems to be boiling.

"Come on boy! Your turn!"

Lucas's tummy then becomes the center of the world. He reveals a muscular body, then slowly lowers his boxers and exhibits a clean-shaven skin and a beautiful cock. *Don't bite your lips, he's your housemate, don't look at him this way...*

A minute later, Lucas seems incapable of repressing a tension that leaves the three of us silent. The shy Cath squeaks, her shirt open on her blue bra, her pants open on her see-through panties. She bites her lips and slips a hand on her stomach before whispering to Mary - without the slightest discretion - that the time has come for her to do her share.

"So? Are you sucking the guy now or waiting for winter to come?"

Mary seems shocked by Cath's provocation, but eventually bites her lips too as Cath begins to gently caress her lower abdomen.

"You said you'd suck him, right?"

"What?! No way! What next??"

Then Cath looks towards me before looking back at a smiling and nodding Mary. *No, no, leave me alone, leave me outside of this, girls…*

"Mary, you could blow Lucas for a while, and then Berenice could take over so everyone would be happy... She's trying to be invisible here but if one of us actually needs a shag here it's her, uh?"

Mary nods, both girls look at me. *No, no way…*

"What?! No way! Leave me out of this!" - *Fuck! Bitches!*

Lucas, watches the match while Mary, obviously pleased with the deal proposed by Cath, gets up to remove her pretty dress under the pretext of avoiding traces. In less time than it is necessary to say, Mary finds herself in her underwear, kneels before an incredulous Lucas, and takes in her right hand the clean-shaven hard cock that soon finishes between her lips.

Cath, the so-called shy girl, seems to have lost all sense of modesty. This girl, usually discreet and prudish, now caresses herself softly, in silence, her thighs spread apart. Lucas, of course, does not lose a crumb of Cath's silent fingering, and occasionally moans as Mary swallows him deeper, more or less silently.

The girls give me a break but the evening has turned wild. I take the opportunity to watch the scene, noticing how excited Mary seems. On her knees and holding Lucas's waist, she moves her mouth and head back and forth on the cock while Lucas tries to keep her hair on the side to enjoy the sight and slides his hands inside her bra, grabs her breasts roughly. *Oh, my, damn it! Go on girl! Don't just stay there, get some of that fun too!*

Without thinking too much, I get up and go to Lucas and Mary. In the utmost silence, I take off my skirt and pullover, and kneel in front of Lucas, beside Mary. *Ok girls, let's do this…*

"You share?"

My left-hand slips into Mary's back, I kiss her cheek, and undertake to help her in her task. Lucas's cock is still in the blond girl's mouth, I push my hair behind my ears and begin to cup his balls with my hand. My other hand moves on his tummy and chest, I bend, undertake to lick the shaft while Mary sucks on the head with passion. I gobble his balls very gently, one after the other, before licking his shaft again, up to the head.

To my surprise, Mary gives me a smile and leaves Lucas' swollen cock, before caressing my hair and guiding him into my mouth. She kisses him, lets her tongue swirl around the head once more, until our tongues meet. Mary looks into my eyes in silence, gently grabs my neck, shares Lucas with me. The hard cock swells in my mouth, I squeak and moan. *Hmmm, I need to do this more often.* Mary nods, as if reading my thoughts.

Mary then looks at Cath, who's trousers are now lying on the floor. The red-head girl's panties are down her legs, she is wide open on the couch, fingering herself and trying to remain as silent as possible, biting her lips with a lusty look. Mary smiles at her, looks at me again as I stroke Lucas and slide him down my throat until my mouth actually touches his base. *Fuck Fuck Fuck I love that cock!!!* I gag, release Lucas, Mary kisses my cheek and gets the man in her mouth again as I catch my breath. Our tongues meet again, mingle around Lucas' burning limb.

Mary settles on the side, plunges her hand between her thighs, looks at Cath who still appears to be very busy.

Lucas gets his hands into my bra, caresses my breasts, pinches my tits until I moan. He then caresses my hair, makes a ponytail, then pushes his cock deep inside my mouth. *He's gonna fuck my mouth...* My tongue brushes it, I tilt my head, welcome this sweet and delicious shaft. *Hmmm, naughty girl, you have to do this kind of thing more often...*

I look up at Lucas, who watches me suck him with pleasure. My lips slide from the base of his cock to the tip of his head, then release it with a kiss, soft and sonorous. *Hmmm, I love it...*

The girls bite their lips, Cath is in a trance, Mary has lost all sense of modesty too. They applaud, look at me with a delighted air. Then Mary whispers.

"Lucas, Berenice would need a little..." - *What???*

"Mary!! You bitch!!"

Lucas does not let me finish my sentence. His cock is on fire, he makes me stand and takes me gently in his arms. He makes me lift my arms up and removes my bra without any delicacy, caresses my breasts before nibbling on my tits. He then takes my hips, flips me around, takes my breasts harder and makes me face the girls who, wide open on the couch, do not lose a crumb of the scene.

Then Lucas's free hand plunges directly into my cotton panties. *Yeah, sorry, not frankly sexy but… Oh come on, fuck me!!!*

The following? Lucas sent my panties to the girls and slipped between my thighs without asking my opinion. But I did nothing to stop him either. A doggy style quickie. Sweet at first, then faster. Silent for starters, then groaning, and finally insanely rough and sonorous.

Lucas came and went, pounded me, made me scream, holding me firmly. The girls watched in silence, facing me and looking straight into my eyes. Lucas, at last, groaned and arched. His cock hit deep inside me, tearing me apart until my orgasm and screams woke the neighbors up. His cum flooded me while his cock kept stretching in me, in violent hits. While I caught my breath, Lucas slipped out of me, kissed my temple and whispered a "we should do that more often, uh?" while the girls applauded happily, delighted to have witnessed this fairly unexpected development.

When I looked-up, the girls looked at me with approval. After a moment of silence, Cath began to blush and dressed-up as best she could, under the taunting jokes of Mary, who was fully enjoying herself. But Lucas was not there anymore, even if his pleasure still leaked on my thighs.

THANK YOU!

This book was my first book published ever, and quite logically the first volume of the '*My Lip-biting Short Stories*' Series.

The three short stories contained in this book have been written with a simple objective in mind, giving the readers a steamy occasion to evade and I am very proud to say that both this book and the series are regularly in the best sellers category, on Amazon.com and Amazon.co.uk.

I do hope that you have enjoyed them and that my ambition has been fulfilled. If so, please leave me some stars and an encouraging comment on Amazon! It helps a lot! Thank you in advance!

[...]

The next volumes of the series contain more or longer short stories, I hope you will enjoy them too! In case you wanted a teaser, just keep turning the pages. But be careful, volume 2 is addictive and a best seller too!

Finally, don't forget to join my mailing list! I will use it to let you know about my future book releases (and subscribers get one of my unpublished sexy stories for free…).

Here is the link:

http://eepurl.com/cQtD_1

Yours,
Alex.

* * *

TEASER
(Abstract from Book 2)

1 AND WHEN YOU'RE DONE...

Don't get me wrong, I love my husband. I really do. But when it comes to sex, things have not been working well enough. I mean, we have sex. Great sex, loving sex. But he and I have very opposite views on the notion of fantasies.

Mine is 'treat me like a queen, fuck me like a whore'. Jonathan treats me like a queen, loves me like a queen, even eats me like a queen, but he refuses to do more. He sees me as a mother, respects women too much to dare...

fucking me nasty. He won't go rough, never. He won't pull my hair, won't push me, won't make me yell, won't play beyond cuddles and loving sex.

So I've decided to, well, get some attention anyway.

I downloaded an app for people looking for dates and left a message there. Different guys replied. Some offered to get brutal. *Really? What's wrong with you people?* Some went on talking and talking. *Nope, thank you...* Others wanted a simple night out. *Still nope, sorry...* Until that guy showed up, looking for the same thing as I did. Well, sort of, obviously. The other way around. His wife would not let him play and he needed... that. He was a bit older, ten years more than me. But banging a younger girl made part of his fantasy. *Why not.*

So we talked. Not too much, just enough to decide. We exchanged a couple of emails, decided to get on a cam, to... well, check each other out. I insisted on doing that in the dark, terrified of being recognized or even recorded, but he undressed, asked to see more skin. And of course, things went a little bit out of control. He got hard staring at my bra, and I got excited looking at his... manhood. And so we both ended up caressing and having fun on our side of the screen. I loved watching him cum, loved knowing I was the cause of that. But after the action, we felt so awkward that we switched off and stopped talking to each other for a while. Silence.

Last week came with a surprise. An email, actually, asking me if I was still interested in doing this. I replied.

We considered our options. I wanted some place neutral yet we didn't want to get this done in a cheap hotel. We talked about taboos and limits too. None for me, I wanted it hard and rough. So did he. Blowjobs? *Hell yes, dirty ones even.* Anal? *Hmmm, that would be a first, we'll see.*

Anyway, we planned a drink and booked a table in a fancy hotel the day after. Which basically is today. Sunday.

I didn't sleep much, felt guilty yet very excited. I went to see my friend Emy to get my legs waxed. And my bikini too, actually. Then I spent an hour choosing my outfit, tried five dresses and ten underwear sets before opting for a white ample skirt and a light shirt. I came back home twice, once after realizing that I forgot to take a condom and another after thinking that maybe one wouldn't be enough.

Then I took a taxi and headed for that bar.

I met him in the street. He kindly helped me get out of the cab. He seemed delicate. Definitely ten years older than me but elegant, with peppery hair. *Hmmm, not bad actually...* He took my arm and brought me inside.

He got me a large seat in the lobby's bar and looked at me as I crossed my legs. Then his eyes dropped into my top, looking for my bra. *Weird at first but... Right, let's open one more button, you're here to fuck me, boy.* My move made him smile. His smile made me bite my lip and giggle. *He's totally gonna fuck me.*

He talked to me for about ten minutes. His

eyes stayed locked on mine. You wouldn't normally sustain that kind of look. Four seconds maybe, five tops. But I played. His eyes explored mine, he eventually started babbling, more focused on my eyes than on his actual conversation. And I wasn't listening anyway.

Then he stood up, came close to me, still looking into my eyes. He checked my legs and boobs on the way, of course, but he made eye contact again. He was so close. I bet I would have heard him whispering despite the noise. He probably would have heard my heart beat, actually. And our eyes made it all. Not even a word.

"I need to have you now."

"I know."

"Wow, your boobs..."

"I know."

"And those legs..."

His hand got on my knee, caressed it gently.

"I know."

"So what do we do now?"

Still, silence, not a single word, his eyes were burning, the room temperature was becoming unbearable. I opened my collar a little more, tried to find some air around. *None, pfieww.* Then our silent eye-to-eye discussion started again.

"So what do we do now, beautiful girl?"

"I don't see too many options here, you're gonna have to do what has to be done..."

[…]

* * *

To be continued in Volume Two of the My Lip-Biting Short Stories Series by Alex Frack.

Available on Amazon of course!

Made in the USA
Monee, IL
02 April 2024

56224328R00038